Bitter Bananas

BY **Isaac Olaleye**

ILLUSTRATED BY **Ed Young**

PUFFIN BOOKS

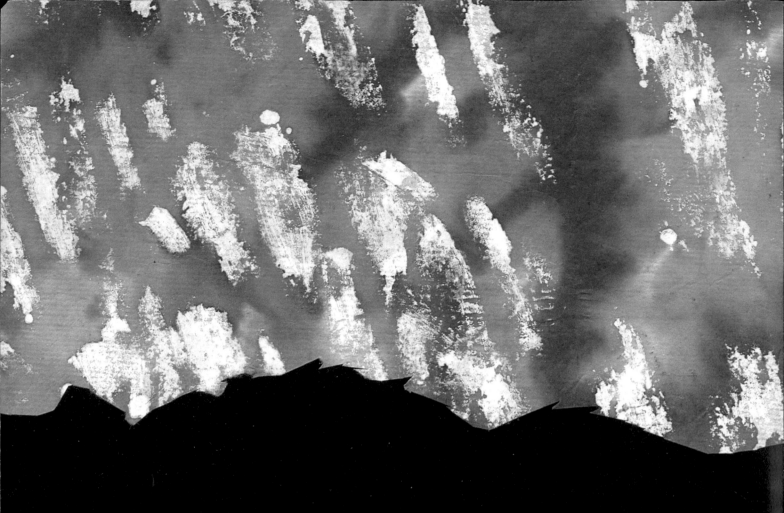

PUFFIN BOOKS
Published by the Penguin Group
Penguin Books USA Inc., 375 Hudson Street, New York, New York 10014, U.S.A.
Penguin Books Ltd, 27 Wrights Lane, London W8 5TZ, England
Penguin Books Australia Ltd, Ringwood, Victoria, Australia
Penguin Books Canada Ltd, 10 Alcorn Avenue, Toronto, Ontario, Canada M4V 3B2
Penguin Books (N.Z.) Ltd, 182-190 Wairau Road, Auckland 10, New Zealand

Penguin Books Ltd, Registered Offices: Harmondsworth, Middlesex, England

First published in the United States of America by Caroline House,
Boyds Mills Press, Inc., A Highlights Company, 1994
Published in Puffin Books, 1996

10 9 8 7 6 5 4 3 2 1

Text copyright © Isaac Olaleye, 1994
Illustrations copyright © Ed Young, 1994
All rights reserved

ISBN 0-14-055710-5

Printed in Hong Kong

Dedicated to the children who will one
day read children's stories to their
children, and to children who will one
day write children's stories — I . O .

To bitter tastes, which reside within all
lasting sweetness — E . Y .

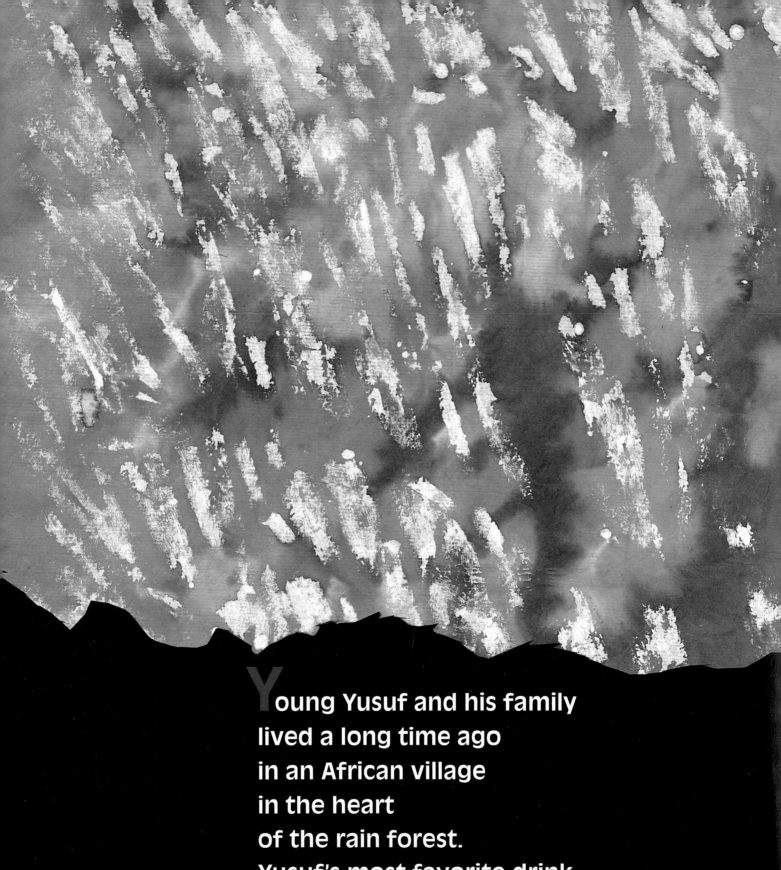

Young Yusuf and his family
lived a long time ago
in an African village
in the heart
of the rain forest.
Yusuf's most favorite drink
was palm sap.
Oh yes! Oh yes!

Now, Yusuf's palm sap,
white as milk,
was sweet like apple juice.

And what he did not drink, young Yusuf sold at the market to help his family.

But somebody was stealing Yusuf's palm sap!
Oh no! Oh no!

One morning
before the first cock crow,

Yusuf hid in the darkness
of the rain forest.

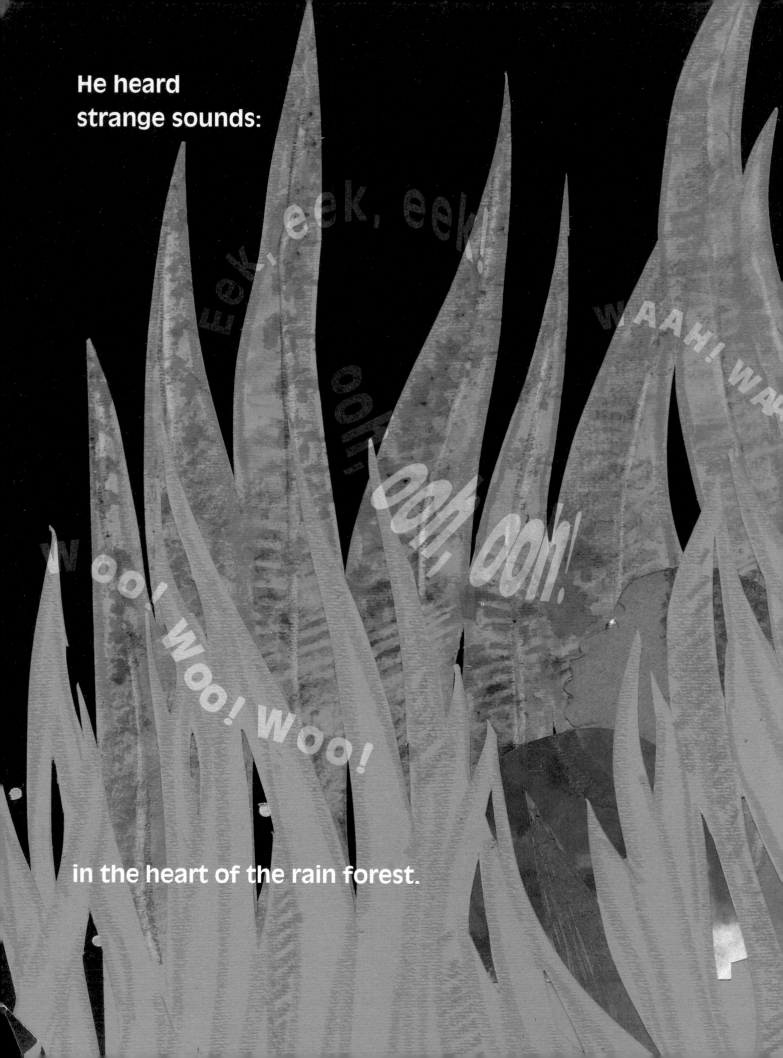

He heard
strange sounds:

in the heart of the rain forest.

He also heard sounds that were not strange:
Bireep, bireep **of croaking frogs.**
And *chir-rup, chir-rup* **of**
chirping crickets.

Gradually the darkness
faded into twilight.
Then Yusuf heard
another very strange sound:
Grr-umph, grr-umph, grr-umph!
Urrp urrp grr-umph urrp!
The sound was moving toward him!
Oh no! Oh no!

Suddenly,
out from the underbrush
they sprang—
papa baboons, mama baboons,
and baby baboons!

"Baboons,
all bibbing my sap!"
cried Yusuf.

Oh no! Oh no!

Yusuf charged out of the bush like a bull.
"Leave my palm sap alone," he yelled.
And the baboons bounded off.

Oh yes! Oh yes!

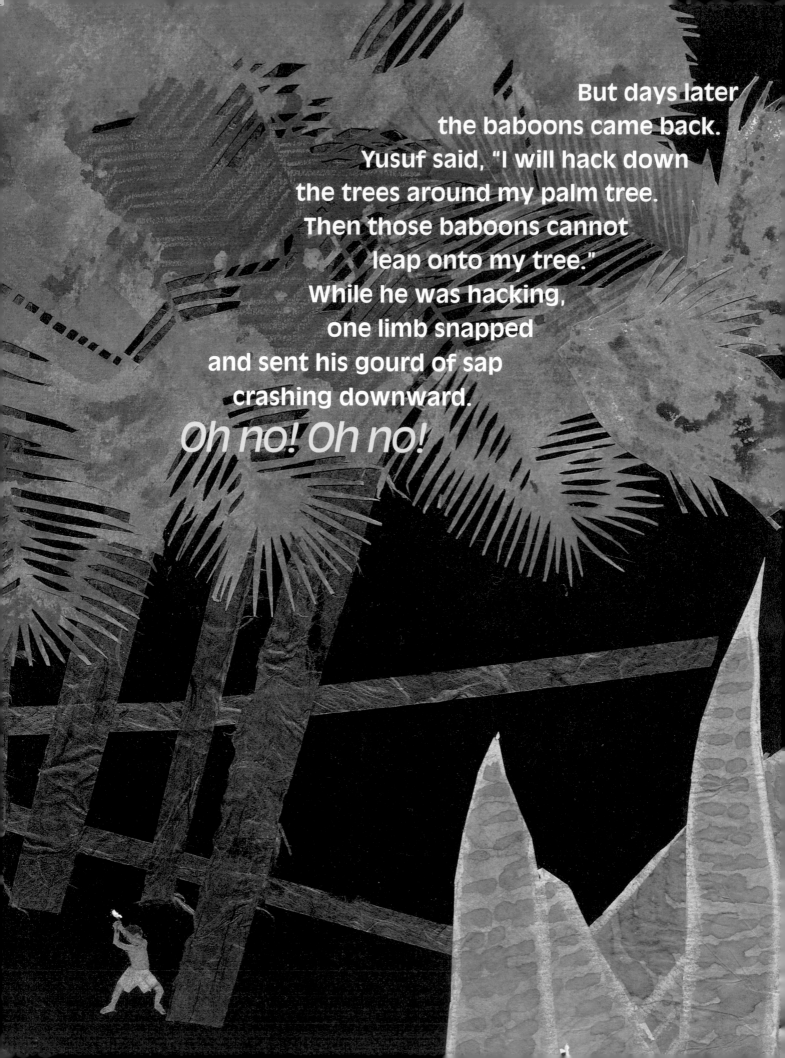

But days later
the baboons came back.
Yusuf said, "I will hack down
the trees around my palm tree.
Then those baboons cannot
leap onto my tree."
While he was hacking,
one limb snapped
and sent his gourd of sap
crashing downward.
Oh no! Oh no!

Yusuf shook his fist
at the palm tree.
"I will scare those baboons,"
Yusuf said.

And so a scarecrow he made.
And the scarecrow
scared the baboons away.
Oh yes! Oh yes!

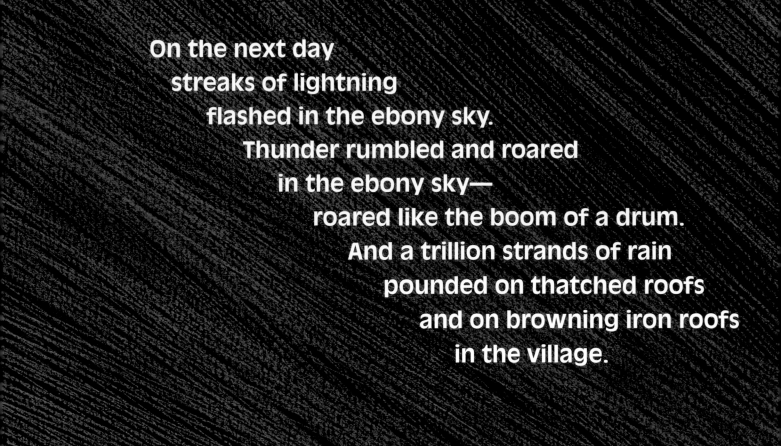

On the next day
   streaks of lightning
      flashed in the ebony sky.
      Thunder rumbled and roared
      in the ebony sky—
         roared like the boom of a drum.
      And a trillion strands of rain
         pounded on thatched roofs
            and on browning iron roofs
            in the village.

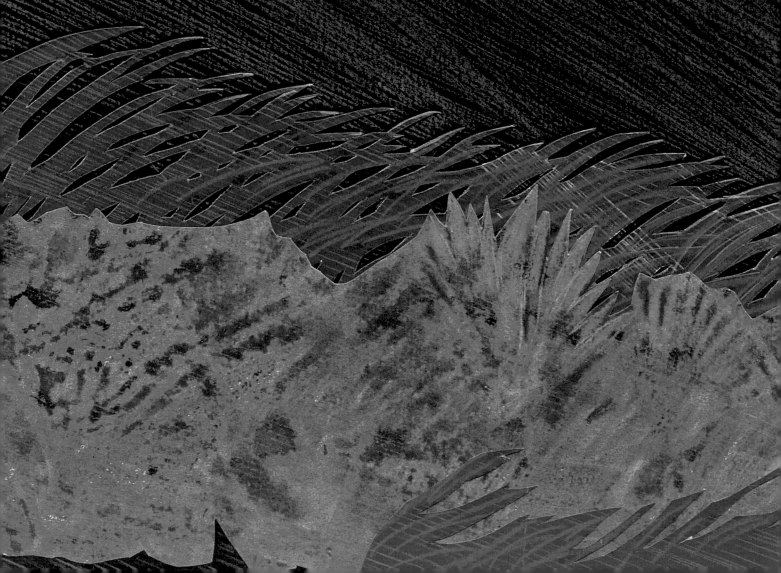

Trees bowed to the wind.
The rain forest wept.
The scarecrow wept.
The wind twisted the scarecrow
and its head flew away in the wind.
Oh no! Oh no!

After the storm,
the baboons were scared no more
and the sweet sap they drank again.
Yusuf cried, "Those baboons
will not make a monkey out of me!"
Suddenly, Yusuf had a very clever idea!

Oh yes! Oh yes!

He dressed up the big gourd
to look like a little boy
with a big tummy and a tiny head
with a knitted cap.
And the baboons
did not sip the sap.

But *"Oh no! Oh no!"*
said Yusuf.
For chirping, twittering,
fluttering birds
liked the knitted cap.
And soon—
the knitted cap was no more!

Yusuf moaned,
"I have no sap to drink.
I have no sap to sell.
What am I going to do now?"
He began to think, think, and think.

"Oh yes! Oh yes!" Yusuf yelled.
"I know . . . I know
what I am going to do."

Three gourds full of palm sap
he bought from the village market.

Four calabash bowls
he got from his mother.

A bunch of ripe bananas
he picked up from a farm.

Some tender wormwood leaves
he plucked from the forest.

In a mortar
he pounded
oozy, mushy,
bitter green juice
from the wormwood leaves.
Palm sap bubbled
like a brook as Yusuf filled
four calabash bowls
with sap bought from the market.

Some green juice
he added to the sap.
Some green juice
he poured into his
own big gourd.

Six heads were needed
to carry everything:
Yusuf's head, his father's,
his mother's, his sister's,
and his two brothers'.
Up, up he climbed
to fasten the big gourd.
Bananas were split open.
Into them he put the green juice.
Bowls were placed at
the foot of the tree.
The job was done.
Oh yes! Oh yes!

The following morning . . .

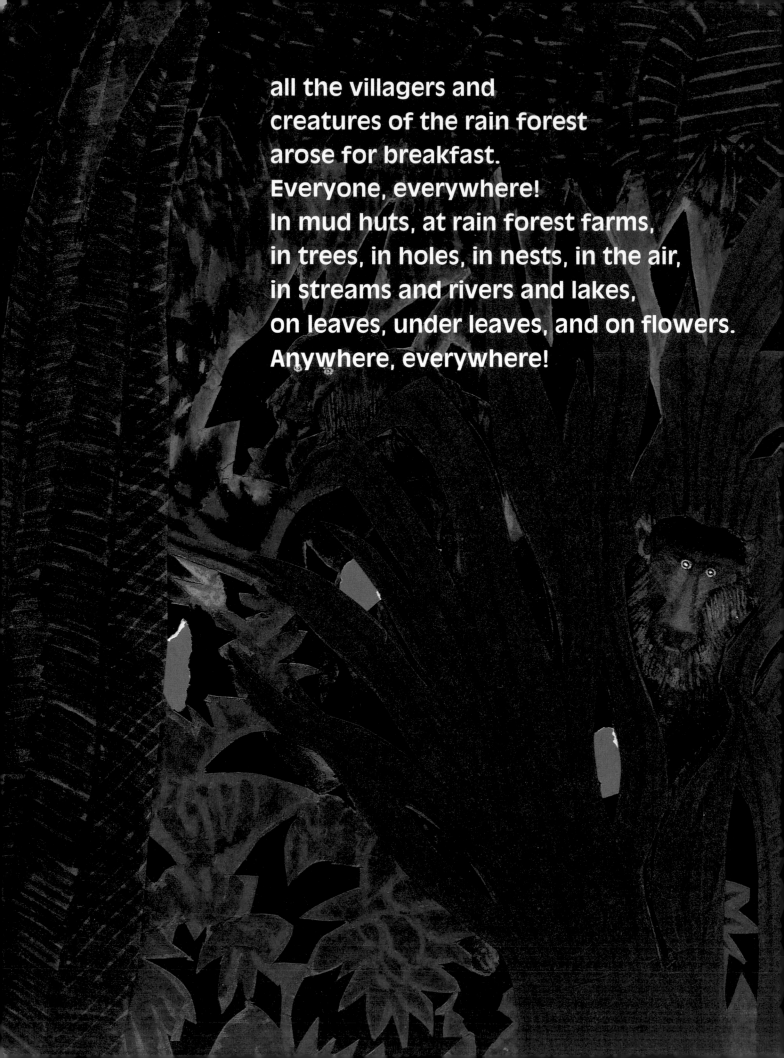

all the villagers and
creatures of the rain forest
arose for breakfast.
Everyone, everywhere!
In mud huts, at rain forest farms,
in trees, in holes, in nests, in the air,
in streams and rivers and lakes,
on leaves, under leaves, and on flowers.
Anywhere, everywhere!

Papa baboons, mama baboons,
and baby baboons, too,
headed for breakfast
at the foot of Yusuf's palm tree!
Oh yes! Oh yes!

The baboons chomped on the bananas.
If baboons could talk
they would have said,
"Bitter bananas!
How are yellow bananas bitter?"
The baboons had
a sip of the sap.
If baboons could talk
they would have said,
"Bitter sap!
How is
sweet palm sap
bitter?"
Then away they went,
as if to say,
"We don't like bitter breakfast!
Oh no! Oh no!"

And they never
came back again.

Yusuf yelled, "Wormwood!

Baboons
do not like
green, oozy,
bitter wormwood juice
in their sap and bananas."

And he did a little joyous,
jumping, jingle jig!
For Yusuf, the end of the matter was sweet!
Really sweet!

Oh yes! Oh yes!

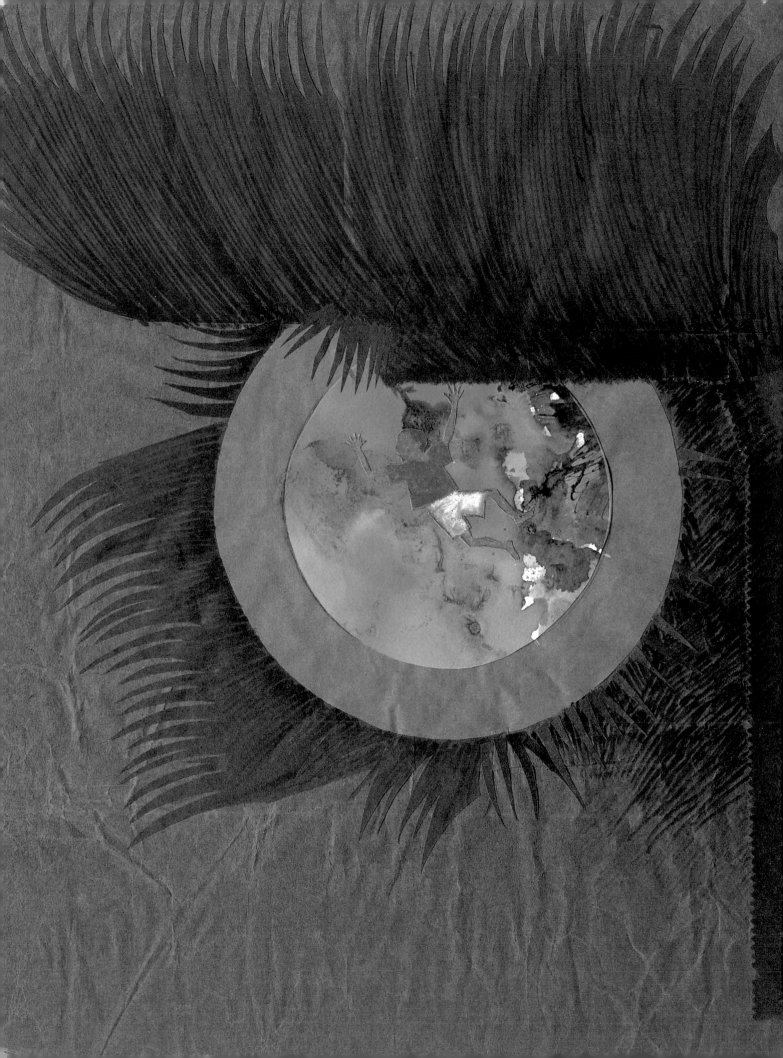